For Sylvie, whose friendship I cherish
Mathilde Stein

For Auke

Mies van Hout

Text copyright © 2006 by Mathilde Stein
Illustrations copyright © 2006 by Mies van Hout
Originally published under the title *Van Mij*
by Lemniscaat b.v. Rotterdam, 2006
All rights reserved
Printed in Belgium
First U.S. edition, 2007

Library of Congress Cataloging-in-Publication Data is available.

LEMNISCAAT
An Imprint of Boyds Mills Press, Inc.
A Highlights Company

815 Church Street
Honesdale, Pennsylvania 18431

Mine!

Mathilde Stein

ILLUSTRATIONS BY Mies van Hout

Lemniscaat
Asheville, North Carolina

One night when Charlotte went to bed, she found a little white ghost under her covers.

"Mine!" he shouted, and he grabbed all the blankets.

"Yours?" Charlotte asked. "This is my bed. You are welcome to stay for a sleepover. But scoot over. Bear has to fit in, too."

The next morning when Charlotte woke up, she heard a cheerful song coming from the bathroom.

The moment she stepped into the tub, the ghost stopped singing. "Mine!" he said grumpily.

Charlotte shrugged. "Could you teach me that song?" she asked.

After the bath, the ghost quickly seated himself on top of the sock pile.

"Mine!"

Charlotte made a face. "Don't be silly. You don't even have feet! Or were you looking for something to wear on your head?"

While Charlotte set the table, the ghost quickly put butter and jelly on all the bread.

"Mine!" he screamed.

Charlotte smiled. "Enjoy your breakfast," she said. "I don't suppose you'll have room for any of this apple pie after you've eaten all those sandwiches. When you're ready, would you like to go outside and play together?"

But the ghost simply did not know how to play with someone else. He would not let go of the swing. He only said, "Mine!"

He would not toss the ball. Instead, he ran away with it and said, "Mine!" And he sat on top of the marbles. "Mine! Mine! Mine!"

Charlotte sighed. "Now listen," she finally said. "If you are going to be like this all day, I'm going to play by myself. Good-bye, ghost."

The ghost looked bashful and quite unhappy.
"Humph," he said. And "Um ..."

After a while, he floated back to Charlotte. He didn't say anything. Secretly he wanted to know how to play with her.

Charlotte showed the ghost different games. They practiced playing all morning and all afternoon. The ghost tried his best. Once he put all the marbles in his pocket—accidentally, of course. And once he held on to the swing a little too tightly.

By the end of the day he could catch and toss
the ball nine times without screaming "Mine!"
"Brilliant!" Charlotte cheered. "Let's celebrate!"

Charlotte made batter, the ghost held the pan, and, together, they made a tall stack of pancakes. They were about to begin eating when the doorbell rang.

"Hello," said a man at the door. "I'm from the castle on the hill. It seems that one of our ghosts has run away. Any chance you have seen him? He is small and white, and he won't share. He doesn't know how to play with others."

Charlotte thought for a minute. "No," she said finally. "I know only one ghost and he is very nice. He turns on the light for you at night, he runs a bath for you. He lays out your socks, and he butters the bread. Besides, he makes wonderful pancakes. Would you like to try one?"

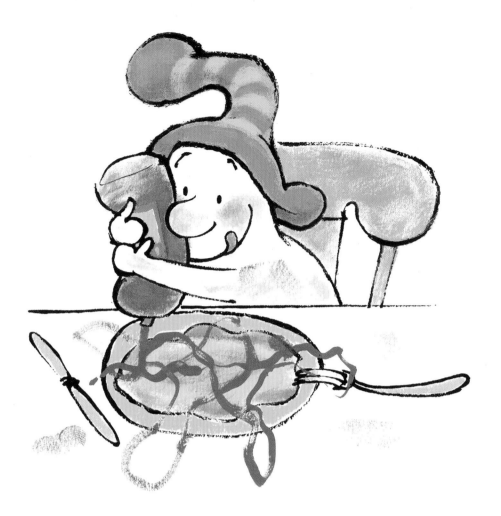

They had a real party. The ghost poured the syrup, and after dinner they danced.

"It's amazing," the man told the ghost. "You look exactly like our ghost, only you are friendlier! It is a pity you're not him. His parents miss him terribly." He coughed. "To be honest, so do I. I hope I will find him soon."

The next morning the ghost was gone.

Charlotte searched the whole house.
"Where are you, ghost? We were going to eat
apple pie, remember? And you can go on the
swings first today."

But the ghost was nowhere to be found.

A few days later an envelope arrived.
"Mine!" it said on the front.

But the drawing inside said "Yours!"